Donnie and his family lived in the city.

But now Donnie and his family
have decided to move to the
country.

Donnie was excited because the new house was right next to a forest that had animals living in it.

From Donnie's new bedroom,
he could see deer.

The next day after the move,
Donnie went outside and sat at
the edge of the forest and
watched the deer.   5

They seemed shy like him. But one deer came close and tried to look Donnie in the eyes with his big brown doe eyes.

6

But Donnie would not look at
the deer, so the deer ran away.

Donnie did not understand why the deer ran away from him, so he got up and sadly walked back to his house.

8

Later, Donnie looked out from his bedroom window and saw all the deer playing with each other.

"Why won't they play with me", he thought. Donnie stared out of his window watching the deer for a long time.

Donnie saw one deer go up to another deer and look him in the eyes. It seemed as if they shared a moment of happiness because each wanted to make a new friend.

After that, Donnie saw the deer
go off to play.

Donnie looked around for
another deer and saw that deer
look into the eyes of another
deer, smile and then go off to
play. They seemed happy to
make a new connection.   13

Donnie laid down on his bed
and tried to figure out what
was going on.

14

Ohhh!!! Each deer looked at each other in the eyes when they first met, feeling happy to make a connection and a new friend. After that they went off to play.

Now Donnie had a plan.

The next day Donnie went back to his spot at the edge of the forest hoping the deer would come back.

He knew it would be hard, but he wanted to show the deer how happy he was to make new friends with them. To do that, he would have to look them in the eyes when they first came up to him.

18

Donnie knew he had to keep his eyes on the deer so the deer would feel safe enough to come up to him. The deer came close to Donnie and laid down on the ground, all the while looking at him and seeing how happy he was.

It was hard for Donnie, but he remained still and kept looking at the beautiful deer even though it felt too difficult at the time.

After a couple minutes, the
deer got up and slowly walked
away. Donnie hoped the deer
would return. 21

Soon after leaving, the deer returned and brought back a group of other deer to meet Donnie.

All the deer saw the joy in
Donnie's eyes as they went
near him, and since Donnie
didn't look away, they came
closer and seemed happy
meeting a new friend. 23

Donnie felt so comfortable and happy with the deer, that he stood up and petted one of the deer on the head.

After a few minutes, Donnie happily skipped back to his house.

Donnie realized he made friends with all these animals by just being his happy self and looking each of them in the eyes and making a connection. Now he would do this with people.   26

The next morning, Donnie went to the house next door where a boy his age was living and knocked on the door.

A boy opened the door and Donnie looked at him with a twinkle in his eyes and said, "Hi, my name is Donnie, do you want to come out and play?"

"Sure" said the boy. "Let's go!"

Made in the USA
Lexington, KY
15 October 2014